www.mascotbooks.com

Sophie & Paige: Soccer Twins

©2015 Joseph Hicks. All Rights Reserved. No part of this publication may be reproduced, stored in a retrieval system or transmitted in any form by any means electronic, mechanical, or photocopying, recording or otherwise without the permission of the author.

All University of Virginia indicia are protected trademarks or registered trademarks University of Virginia and are used under license.

For more information, please contact:
Mascot Books
560 Herndon Parkway #120
Herndon, VA 20170
info@mascotbooks.com

CPSIA Code: PRT1115A
ISBN-13: 978-1-63177-327-3

Printed in the United States

Sophie & Paige
SOCCER TWINS
by Joseph Hicks

Foreword

Whether you are part of a team, a classroom, a family, or a society, one of the best lessons you can learn is how to serve one another. Sophie and Paige helped one another improve and in turn they helped themselves. The greatest reward you can give yourself is to help someone grow and reach their dreams.

Steve Swanson
University of Virginia Women's Soccer Coach
World Champion USWNT Assistant Coach

Acknowledgements

For their caring and generosity, I would like to acknowledge the following individuals. Without them, this book would never have happened!

Chrissy Ouellette, Leah Pugh, Ashley Jenkins, Connie Sword, Mary Lynn Putney, Paul McCaffery, Sofia, Ellie, and Peralta, Keri Wein, Stephanie Sztan, Bruce Russell, Alec Hauser, Jack Moores, Ann Moores, Reid and Clare Strassheim, Carrie Heilman, Owen and Lily Sexton, Lesley Hicks, Sherry Newton Strauss, and Marcus Sparks.

A special shout-out to:

Steve Swanson for providing the foreword

4 Sporty Girls, positive and empowering girls' apparel- 4sportygirls.com

Hans Hobson and staff at Tennessee State Soccer Association

Jean and Tommy Soehn at Kick Like A Girl- kicklikeagirl.com

On the outside, Paige and Sophie are identical.

But on the inside, they are very different.

Paige was a soccer star! She was quick at learning to kick the ball. She was graceful when she dribbled.

In school, Paige was not a star. She was a slow reader. Her letters were clumsy and were rarely in the right place.

Sophie was a school star! She was a speedy reader. Her letters and words fit together beautifully.

But at soccer practice, Sophie was not a star. She was sluggish when she ran. When she played, her feet did crazy things.

During homework time, Sophie flies through her reading and muscles through her math.

During homework time, Paige trips over the words and stumbles over the numbers.

After homework time, Paige and Sophie play soccer. Paige flies through the yard and muscles the ball into the goal.

Sophie trips over the ball and stumbles over her own feet.

On soccer days, Paige is a shining star.

Sophie is a gloomy glump.

On report card days, Sophie
is a shimmering sunflower.
Paige is a murky mushroom.

The twins made a plan!
Paige will help Sophie with soccer.
Sophie will help Paige with school.

"What an idea!" bubbled Paige. "I'll show you
how to run like a champ. I can show you how
to kick like a pro!"

"I can teach you how to read like an ace. I
can teach you how to multiply like a maniac!"
cheered Sophie.

Paige and Sophie stuck to their plan.
As they grew up, Paige improved in school.
She no longer tripped over numbers.

Sophie got better at soccer. She no longer stumbled over her own feet.

At college, Paige could play on a victorious soccer team *and* be a student.

At college, Sophie could be a champion student *and* play some soccer.

College work was tough for Paige. Sometimes homework made her tug at her ponytail.

College soccer was rough for Sophie.
Sometimes practice made her legs feel like jelly.

Paige taught Sophie fancier ways to kick the ball. She showed her how to eat healthy so her legs would have more energy.

Sophie taught Paige how to study smarter. She showed her how to relax so her brain would have more energy.

KLOCKNER STADIUM

Sophie became a much better soccer player.
The crowd would roar when she played!

Paige became a much better student. Her
mom would roar when her report card came!

Not long after this, both Paige and Sophie graduated with honors! It was time for them to decide what they wanted to do. They were both sporty and intelligent, so they had many choices. But for them, it wasn't a hard decision!

One of them became a famous author.
She wrote books people couldn't stop reading!

BOOK SIGNING

One of them became an Olympic soccer player. When she played, people couldn't stop cheering!

About the Author

Joseph Hicks was born in the small town of Richlands, Virginia. He spent his childhood running barefoot through the woods along the banks of the Clinch River. Snake hunts, imaginary sword fights, and digging for buried treasure filled his days on his quest to find the power of Greyskull. That is, until one day, his mom encouraged him to lace up his tennis shoes and meet her on the tennis court, which spurred a new passion for Joseph. So began his love of sports, competition, and the thrill of being average.

Joseph learned that dedication and long hours of practice didn't always equal victory, finding this to be true both on the court and in the classroom. After many years of academic and athletic struggles, he realized that his failures were actually strengthening him from within, for he gained patience, humility, and an unrelenting sense of optimism.

Joseph attributes his parents for allowing him to explore the freedoms of childhood while raising him to see the value of kindness and cooperation. Over twenty years later, Joseph now lives in Charlottesville, Virginia with his wife Lesley and their soccer star daughter Sophie. While his quest for Greyskull remains alive and well, his new passion involves inspiring and educating young minds in the classroom.

In 2011, Joseph published his first children's fantasy novel entitled, *The Virginia Underground*. It was met with rave reviews from fantasy fans from coast-to-coast. It was quickly followed up by its sequel, *The Tennessee Underground*.

Joseph encourages all of you, his readers and his students, to take your setbacks and failures in stride because make no mistake, there is a flower that's blooming inside of you, and when it sees the light of day, the world had better watch out!

If you love the book, please "like" Joseph's Facebook Fanpage (Joseph B. Hicks Fanpage) and follow him on Twitter: @SoccerstarHicks.

Questions for the author? You may also email him directly: josephbhicks@aol.com.